CAN YOU FIND?

TEDDY GOES TO THE PICNIC

© Published by Peter Haddock Ltd., Bridlington
England. Printed in Belgium.
Illustrated by Jane Winton.

Teddy is excited because today

...e day of the teddy-bears' picnic.

He packs his baske

ith his favourite food.

Then he sets off dow

he lane to the woods.

He meets som

friends on the way.

Having reached the woods, the

it down and enjoy their picnic.

They have eaten so muc

hat they all fall asleep.

After they have rested it

'me to play some games.

Teddy is very happ

he has won a prize.

Can you find all thes

hings in this book?